Mavis,

Never stop imagining!

♡ Angela Taylor Hylland

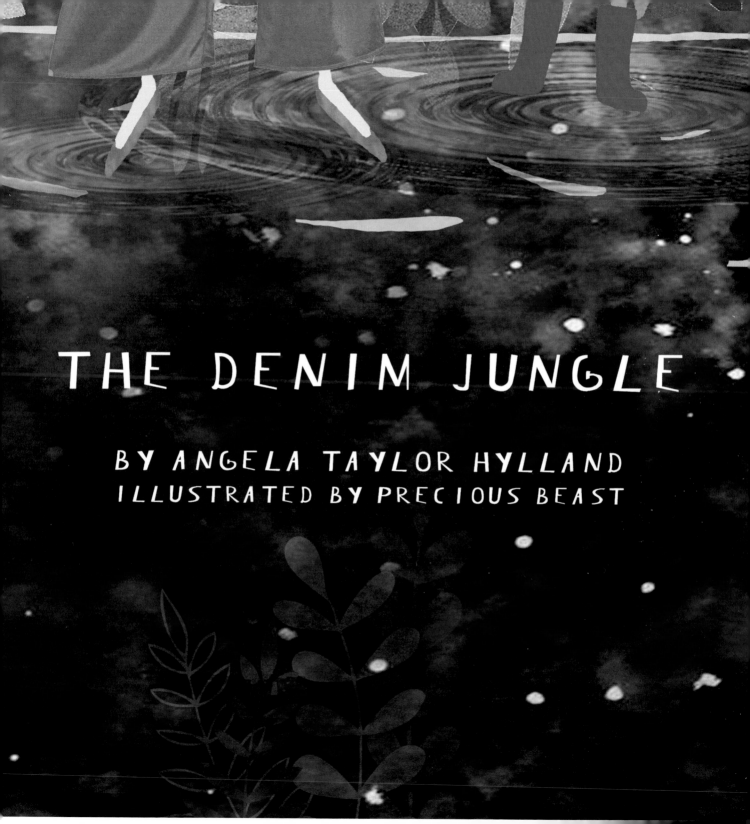

THE DENIM JUNGLE

BY ANGELA TAYLOR HYLLAND
ILLUSTRATED BY PRECIOUS BEAST

To the beats of my heart, Szaba and Von, and to my mother-in-law, Sue, who gifted me this dream.

A special thank you to my husband, Ryan, who revealed the Denim Jungle to his mom all those years ago and has served as my trusted compass on this journey.

Thanks also to Jackie, Shanon, Matt, Catherine, Christa, Deborah, Geraldine, Jason, Jen, Kerry, Keryn, Nate, Patti, Shannon, and Wendy who helped make this spark of an idea really shine.

Copyright © 2015 by Angela Taylor Hylland

Printed in the United States of America

First Printing, 2015

978-0-9969898-0-0

My Castle Heart Publications
1125 N 77th Street
Seattle, WA 98103

www.MyCastleHeart.com

"CAN YOU SEE IT?"
LEO ASKED.

A BUSY
CROWD
SQUEEZED
PAST
(AND FAST).

HIS MOTHER STOOPED TO LEO'S HEIGHT WITH **LEGS** THE ONLY THING IN SIGHT.

STRETCHED
BEFORE THEM,
IT WAS THERE!
A DENIM JUNGLE
. . . EVERYWHERE!

HORDES OF LEGGY, MOVING TREES. TRUNKS OF ANKLES, CALVES, AND KNEES.

MOSTLY DENIM,
MOSTLY BLUE,
QUICKLY
MARCHING
TWO BY TWO.

IN A HURRY,
OFF THEY GO.
BARELY SEEING
THAT BELOW. . .

WONDERS WAIT
TO BE EXPLORED,
DEEP AMID THE
JUNGLE FLOOR.

RIVET BUGS
(ONE METAL EYE)
WATCH AND WINK
AT PASSERSBY.

WHILE NEARBY, PERCHED
IN POCKET NESTS,
CELL PHONE BIRDS
MAKE NOISY GUESTS.

AND CLIMBING DOWN EACH JUNGLE STEM,

A
STEALTHY
SNAKE
HUNTS
DOWN
A HEM.

WHILE PINECONE SOLDIERS
CLOAKED IN
ARMOR,

TRACK A
FLEETING
FAIRY CHARMER...

TO TRAILS OF SNAILS
KEEPING PACE

IN THE SIDEWALK'S
SLOWEST
RACE.

AND DOWN A MOAT,
A FEATHER BOAT

CHARTS
ITS
COURSE
BY
SCRIBBLED
NOTE.

THEN DRIP
DRIP
DROP,
THE
JUNGLE
RAIN

SENDS THEM ALL
BACK HOME AGAIN.

AND
PUDDLE
WINDOWS
LOOK RIGHT
THROUGH THE
GROUND BACK TO
A TREETOP VIEW.

THE WORLD IS MAGIC
HERE BELOW,
BUT THOSE ABOVE
MAY NEVER KNOW.

SO LET'S REMEMBER,
YOU AND I,

TO SEE THE WORLD,
NOT PASS IT BY.

A JUNGLE WAITS BEYOND THIS BOOK...

The Story Behind the Story

Once upon a time, a little boy (my husband, Ryan) told his mom that he felt he was living in a Denim Jungle, surrounded by jean-clad legs towering above.

His mom, Sue, held onto this idea for 30 years, convinced that *The Denim Jungle* would make a memorable kids' book with a sweet message for adults, too.

Months after my first child (Sue's granddaughter) was born, Sue lost her long, valiant battle with breast cancer. Before she left, she entrusted her Denim Jungle dream to me, her daughter-in-law, "the writer."

But we all know the best children's books are as much about the pictures as the story. So I enlisted the help of Jackie Phillips of Precious Beast to bring *The Denim Jungle* from words to *world*.

I humbly hope we've made Sue's dream come true, just as she made so many dreams come true with her open-armed love, cheerleading, and support.

I now leave you with this fairytale ending...

Dream. Reach out. Imagine. Believe. Take time to enjoy the little things—because in the end, they're really the big things.

Angela

CPSIA information can be obtained
at www.ICGtesting.com
Printed in the USA
LVXC02n1359231115
463573LV00008B/22